Dear Parents:

Congratulations! Your child is taking the first steps on an exciting journey. The destination? Independent reading!

STEP INTO READING® will help your child get there. The program offers five steps to reading success. Each step includes fun stories and colorful art or photographs. In addition to original fiction and books with favorite characters, there are Step into Reading Non-Fiction Readers, Phonics Readers and Boxed Sets, Sticker Readers, and Comic Readers—a complete literacy program with something to interest every child.

Learning to Read, Step by Step!

Ready to Read   Preschool–Kindergarten
• big type and easy words • rhyme and rhythm • picture clues
For children who know the alphabet and are eager to begin reading.

Reading with Help   Preschool–Grade 1
• basic vocabulary • short sentences • simple stories
For children who recognize familiar words and sound out new words with help.

Reading on Your Own   Grades 1–3
• engaging characters • easy-to-follow plots • popular topics
For children who are ready to read on their own.

Reading Paragraphs   Grades 2–3
• challenging vocabulary • short paragraphs • exciting stories
For newly independent readers who read simple sentences with confidence.

Ready for Chapters   Grades 2–4
• chapters • longer paragraphs • full-color art
For children who want to take the plunge into chapter books but still like colorful pictures.

STEP INTO READING® is designed to give every child a successful reading experience. The grade levels are only guides; children will progress through the steps at their own speed, developing confidence in their reading. The F&P Text Level on the back cover serves as another tool to help you choose the right book for your child.

Remember, a lifetime love of reading starts with a single step!

For Charlie and Elinor,
who never let fear get
in their way

Copyright © 2018 by Tad Hills
All rights reserved. Published in the United States by Random House Children's Books,
a division of Penguin Random House LLC, New York.
Step into Reading, Random House, and the Random House colophon are registered
trademarks of Penguin Random House LLC.
Visit us on the Web!
StepIntoReading.com
rhcbooks.com
Educators and librarians, for a variety of teaching tools, visit us at RHTeachersLibrarians.com
Library of Congress Cataloging-in-Publication Data is available upon request.
ISBN 978-1-5247-7347-2 (trade) — ISBN 978-1-5247-7348-9 (lib. bdg.)
ISBN 978-1-5247-7349-6 (ebook)
Printed in the United States of America
10 9 8 7 6 5 4 3 2 1
This book has been officially leveled by using the F&P Text Level Gradient™ Leveling System.

Rocket the Brave!

Tad Hills

Random House 🏠 New York

There is a butterfly
on Rocket's nose.

"Hello, butterfly,"

says Rocket.

He wags his tail.

The butterfly flies away.

"Wait," Rocket says.

Rocket is fast.

The butterfly is faster.

The butterfly flies
up the hill.

Rocket runs
up the hill.

The butterfly flies
past the pond.

Rocket runs
past the pond.

The butterfly rests
on a flower.

Rocket rests, too.

The butterfly flies off.

"Wait!" Rocket says.

The butterfly flies
into the forest.

Rocket stops.

The forest is very dark.

The trees are very tall.

Rocket does not
want to go
into the forest.

"The forest is
very scary,"
he says to himself.

Rocket thinks
for a moment.

The butterfly
was not afraid
to go
into the forest.

The butterfly was brave.

Maybe the forest
is not scary.

Rocket walks

into the forest.

It is very dark.

It is very quiet.

There are many
tall trees.

There are
pinecones,

and ferns,

and . . .

the butterfly!

"Hello, butterfly,"
says Rocket.

The forest is
not so scary
after all.

Rocket likes the forest.

Rocket is brave.